CAN YOU SURVIVE THE GRIMMS' FAIRY TALES?

original version by
Jacob and Wilhelm Grimm
adapted by Ryan Jacobson

Minneapolis, Minnesota

DEDICATION

For Lora, Jonah, and Lucas—my happily ever after.

ACKNOWLEDGMENTS

Special thanks to my family and friends for all of your love, support, and patience while I toiled away on this book (and so many others).

Disclaimer: By using this book, including the STEM activity herein, you expressly agree to do so at your sole risk, and you assume full responsibility. You understand and agree that neither Lake 7 Creative, LLC; Ryan Jacobson; nor anyone else involved with this book is responsible or liable for any claim, loss, or damage resulting from the use of this book.

Edited by Emily Beaumont.
Cover art by Margaret Amy Salter. All interior art by Kat Baumann, except book (pg. 6) licensed from Natykach Nataliia/shutterstock.com.

LEXILE®, the LEXILE® logo and POWERV® are trademarks of MetaMetrics, Inc., and are registered in the United States and abroad. Copyright © 2024 MetaMetrics, Inc. All rights reserved.

10 9 8 7 6 5 4 3 2 1

Dear Reader,

I have always loved fairy tales. As a young child, I'd listen to them on our family's record player, or I'd sit down in front of the TV and watch *Shelley Duvall's Faerie Tale Theatre.* And, of course, I watched all the Disney movies: *Cinderella, Sleeping Beauty, Snow White and the Seven Dwarfs,* and so on.

What I didn't know about those Disney movies, until years later, is that they were much less dark and twisted than the original fairy tales upon which they're based. If you haven't ever read the *Grimms' Fairy Tales,* you might be in for a few surprises in the pages ahead. Some moments are shocking and unexpected, while others are kind of funny.

Adapting this collection of short stories into one longer adventure proved to be quite challenging—but that made it one of the most fun adaptations I've ever done. Unfortunately, I couldn't use all the Grimms' fairy tales, so I picked a few of my all-time favorites.

When you're ready to do so, I encourage you to read the original *Grimms' Fairy Tales.* Until then, I hope you find this version to be a magical experience!

—Ryan Jacobson

HOW TO USE THIS BOOK

As you read *Can You Survive the Grimms' Fairy Tales?*, you will sometimes be asked to jump to a distant page. Please follow these instructions. Sometimes you will be asked to choose between two or more options. Decide which you feel is best, and go to the corresponding page. (But be careful; some of the options will lead to disaster.) Finally, if a page offers no instructions or choices, simply go to the next page. Enjoy the story, and good luck!

* * *

Ryan's Notes: *The Grimms' Fairy Tales* are much darker than you might expect, and the content can be disturbing. Please be advised that there are moments of violence. As one example, a witch tries to cook and eat children. As another example, a character decides to chop off her big toe. If this type of content might make you uncomfortable, you may prefer to read a different book instead.

Some language, punctuation, and word choices may seem odd. This is because I did my best to remain true to the original translation from which I worked.

TABLE OF CONTENTS

ONCE UPON A TIME

It is the peculiar glow that startles you awake. Your room should be dark, and you should be asleep—for it is the middle of the night. Yet this strange brightness has your eyes wide open.

You decide that you must be dreaming, for the glow emanates from a woman. She is young and kind-looking; she reminds you of a schoolteacher. But she is no ordinary person. Not only does she glow brightly, but she also floats beside your bed.

You live in a country a great ways off, during a time long ago. It is a land of castles, kings, and queens—and there are in these days fairies. Perhaps this woman before you is just such a creature.

You are a poor child, without parents and without a home. You sleep anywhere you find shelter, and you eat whatever food you can catch or steal. On this night, you are stowed away inside the empty room of the Hanau Inn. You were fortunate to find an unlocked door—or so you think.

"It was not fortune that brought you here," says the woman. "Fate has chosen you for a perilous quest. My name is Allerleirauh. Our world of magic is unraveling; our reality crumbles. Only you can put it right again."

"Me?" you ask. "I'm no one special."

She smiles kindly. "Ah, but you are wrong, young one. This may seem an ordinary room in an ordinary inn. Yet only the one with the purest of hearts and the sharpest of minds could be granted entry. You, my child, were destined to find this place. Now, you are destined to save us all."

You shake your head in disbelief. "How can this be true? I have nothing."

"Everything you need lies within you—well, nearly everything. The other tools you require will be provided throughout your quest. I shall help you, wherever I can, along the way. Look out for magical golden items during your journey. Collect them when you are able. Use them wisely, when the time is right. Bring the rest to me— most importantly, bring me the golden ring."

"But—" you begin to say.

"Our time is short," Allerleirauh interrupts. "Be on your way, and good luck."

"On my way . . . where?" you ask.

She slowly waves her hand, and two flowers appear. "That is for you to decide," she says. "Simply choose a flower, and hold it up."

A red flower.

GO TO PAGE 63.

A purple flower.

GO TO PAGE 20.

You run from the path into the wood to look for flowers. And whenever you pick one, you fancy that you see a still prettier one farther on and run after it—and so go deeper and deeper into the wood. You even find a **GOLDEN FLOWER**.

When you have gathered so many flowers that you can carry no more, you remember you're lost and alone. You set out toward you know not where.

GO TO PAGE 40.

Hearing of the bargain these men want to make, you creep up your father's coat to his shoulder and whisper in his ear, "Take the money, Father, and let them have me. I'll soon come back to you."

The woodman at last says he will sell you for a large piece of gold, and they pay the price. Your father kindly flicks off a speck of GOLDEN DUST and hands it to you. It is like having your own piece of gold.

"Where would you like to sit?" says one of the men.

"Oh, put me on the rim of your hat. That will be a nice gallery for me. I can walk about there and see the country as we go along."

So they do as you wish, and they take you with them.

You journey on till it begins to be dusky, and then you say, "Let me get down. I'm tired."

So the man takes off his hat and puts you down on a clod of earth, in a plowed field by the side of the road. But you run about amongst the furrows and at last slip into an old mouse-hole.

"Goodbye, my masters!" you say. "I'm off! Mind and look sharp after me the next time."

Then they run at once to the place and poke the ends of their sticks into the mouse-hole—but all in vain. You only crawl farther and farther in.

At last, it becomes quite dark, so they are forced to go their way without their prize, as sulky as can be.

When they are gone, you come out of your hiding-place. "What dangerous walking it is, in this plowed field! If I were to fall from one of these great clods, I should undoubtedly break my neck."

At last, by good luck, you find a large, empty snail-shell and sneak inside. "This is lucky," you say. "I can sleep here very well."

Just as you are falling asleep, you hear two men passing by, chatting together.

One says to the other, "How can we rob that rich parson's house of his silver and gold?"

"I'll tell you!" you cry.

"What noise was that?" says the thief, frightened. "I'm sure I heard someone speak."

They stand still, listening, and you say, "Take me with you. I'll show you how to get the parson's money."

"But where are you?" they say.

"Look about on the ground," you answer, "and listen where the sound comes from."

At last the thieves find you out and lift you up in their hands. "You little man!" they say. "What can you do for us?"

"Why, I can get between the iron window-bars of the parson's house and throw you out whatever you want."

"That's a good thought," say the thieves. "Come along. We shall see what you can do."

When you come to the parson's house, you slip through the window-bars into the room and then call out as loud as you can, "Will you have all that is here?"

At this, the thieves are frightened and say, "Softly, softly! Speak low, so you may not awaken anybody."

But you seem as if you did not understand them and bawl out again, "How much will you have? Shall I throw it all out?"

The thieves are frightened and run off. But at last they pluck up their hearts and say, "The little urchin is only trying to make fools of us." So they come back and whisper softly to you, "Now let us have no more of your roguish jokes, but throw us out some of the money."

Then you call out as loud as you can, "Very well! Hold your hands! Here it comes."

In the next room, the cook hears this, so she springs out of bed and runs to open the door. The thieves run off as if a wolf is at their tails.

The cook, having found nothing, goes away for a light. By the time she comes back, you have slipped off into the barn. When she has looked about and searched every hole and corner, she goes to bed.

You crawl about in the hay-loft and at last find a snug place to finish your night's rest. So you lie down, meaning to sleep till daylight and then find your way home to your father and mother.

But, alas, how woefully you are undone! The cook gets up early, before daybreak, to feed the cows. Going straight to the hay-loft, she carries away a large bundle of hay, with you in the middle of it, fast asleep.

You do not wake till you find yourself in the mouth of the cow—for the cook put the hay into the cow's rick, and the cow has taken you up in a mouthful of it. You are forced to have all of your wits about you, that you might not get between the cow's teeth and so be crushed to death.

At last, down you go into her stomach.

"It is rather dark," you say. "They forgot to build windows in this room to let the sun in. A candle would be no bad thing."

You make the best of your bad luck, but you do not like your quarters at all. The worst of it is that more and more hay is always coming down, and the space left for you becomes smaller and smaller.

At last, you cry out as loud as you can, "Don't bring me any more hay! Don't bring me any more hay!"

You hear the cook just then. She must have been milking the cow, for now she runs off as fast as she can to her master the parson and says, "Sir, the cow is talking!"

But the parson says, "You are surely mad!" However, he goes with her into the cow-house, to try and see what is the matter.

You call out, "Don't bring me any more hay!"

Then the parson himself is frightened. Thinking the cow is surely bewitched, he has her killed on the spot. The cow is cut up, and the stomach, in which you lie, is thrown out upon a dunghill.

GO TO THE NEXT PAGE.

You soon set yourself to work to get out, which is not a very easy task. But, at last, just as you have made room to get your head out, fresh ill-luck befalls you. A hungry wolf springs out and swallows up the whole stomach, with you in it, at one gulp, and runs away.

Yes.

GO TO PAGE 74.

No.

GO TO PAGE 23.

You leave a light burning and hide yourselves in a closet, near your workbench, where you'll watch what happens. At least, that is the plan.

As you pull the door almost to closing, it slips from your hand. The door shuts all the way, and you hear a loud *click*. You quickly grab the handle and try to spin it, but the handle does not turn. The door is locked, and you are trapped inside the closet.

As soon as it is midnight, there come sounds of movement from your bench.

Your mysterious shoemakers are here.

You and your wife begin hammering on the door, crying, "Help us! Help us!"

The response you hear is a startled shriek, followed by the pattering of feet running away from your bench and out of your home.

They are gone—and with them goes your only hope of rescue. You and your wife are prisoners inside your own locked closet. And there the two of you will stay.

GO TO PAGE 75.

Like a sudden gust of wind, you feel magic pass through you. And what the little fish had foretold soon comes to pass: The queen has a little girl—and that little girl is you. The king cannot cease looking at you for joy and says he will hold a great feast and show you to all the land. So he invites his kinsmen and nobles and friends and neighbors.

The queen says, "I will have the fairies also, so they might be kind and good to our little daughter."

Now there are 13 fairies in the kingdom. But since the king and queen have only 12 golden dishes for them to eat out of, they are forced to leave one of the fairies without asking her. So 12 fairies come, each with a high red cap on her head and red shoes with high heels on her feet and a long white wand in her hand.

After the feast, the fairies gather around in a ring and give all their best gifts to you. One gives you goodness, another beauty, another riches, and so on till you have all that is good in the world.

Just as 11 of the fairies have finished blessing you, a great noise is heard in the courtyard. Word is brought that the 13th fairy has come, with a black cap on her head and black shoes on her feet and a broomstick in her hand.

Presently, up she comes into the dining-hall. Now, as she has not been asked to the feast, she is very angry and scolds the king and queen very much. She sets to work to take her revenge.

She cries out, "The king's daughter shall, in her 15th year, be wounded by a spindle and fall down dead."

Then the 12th of the friendly fairies, who has not yet given her gift, comes forward and says, "The evil wish must be fulfilled, but I can soften its mischief."

So her gift is that you, when the spindle wounds you, should not really die but should only fall asleep for 100 years.

However, the king still hopes to save you, his dear child, altogether from the threatened evil. So he orders that all the spindles in the kingdom should be bought up and burned.

GO TO THE NEXT PAGE.

In the meantime, all the gifts of the first 11 fairies are fulfilled. You are so beautiful and well behaved and good and wise that everyone who knows you loves you.

It happens that, on the very day you are 15 years old, the king and queen are not at home. You are left alone in the palace. So you rove about and look at all the rooms and chambers, till at last you come to an old tower. There is a narrow staircase leading upward and a wider staircase leading downward.

Go up the stairs.

GO TO PAGE 32.

Go down the stairs.

GO TO PAGE 44.

RAPUNZEL

You are certainly no king, but you are a good man. You have long in vain wished for a child. You and your wife hope that God will grant your desire.

From a little window at the back of your house, a splendid garden can be seen. It is full of the most beautiful flowers and herbs. It is, however, surrounded by a high wall. No one dares to go into it because it belongs to an enchantress, who has great power and is dreaded by all the world.

One day, your wife is standing by this window, looking down into the garden. She sees a bed which is planted with the most beautiful rampion (rapunzel). It looks so fresh and green that she longs for it. She quite pines away and begins to look pale and miserable.

Alarmed, you ask, "What ails you, dear wife?"

"Ah," she replies, "if I can't eat some of the rampion, which is in the garden behind our house, I shall die."

You love her, so you think, *Sooner than let my wife die, I will bring her some of the rampion—let it cost what it will.*

At twilight, you clamber over the wall, into the garden of the enchantress. You hastily clutch a handful of rampion and take it to your wife. She at once makes herself a salad of it and eats it greedily.

It tastes so good to her—so very good—that the next day she longs for it three times as much as before. If you are to have any rest, you must once more descend into the garden.

* * *

In the gloom of evening, you let yourself down again. But when you have clambered down the wall, you are terribly afraid, for you see the enchantress standing before you.

"How can you dare," she says with an angry look, "descend into my garden and steal my rampion like a thief? You shall suffer for it!"

"Ah," you answer, "let mercy take the place of justice.

I only made up my mind to do it out of necessity. My wife saw your rampion from the window and felt such a longing for it that she would have died if she had not got some to eat."

Then the enchantress allows her anger to soften and says, "If the case be as you say, I will allow you to take away with you as much rampion as you will. Only I make one condition: If your wife brings a child into the world, you must give me the child. It shall be well treated, and I will care for it like a mother."

Oh, what a choice! Should you agree to give up your child—one that you might never have? Or will you refuse the enchantress and face the consequence?

What will you choose to do?

Accept the deal.

GO TO PAGE 69.

Refuse the deal.

GO TO PAGE 46.

You are still not disheartened. Thinking the wolf will not dislike having some chat with you, you call out, "My good friend, I can show you a famous treat."

"Where's that?" says the wolf.

"In such and such a house," you say, describing your own father's house.

"You can crawl through the drain into the kitchen and then into the pantry. There, you will find cakes, ham, beef, cold chicken, roast pig, apple-dumplings, and everything that your heart can wish."

The wolf does not want to be asked twice, so that very night he goes to the house and crawls through the drain into the kitchen and then into the pantry. He eats and drinks there to his heart's content.

As soon as he has had enough, he wants to get away. But he has eaten so much that he cannot go out by the same way he came in.

This was just what you had reckoned upon. Now you set up a great shout, making all the noise you can.

"Will you be easy?" says the wolf. "You'll awaken everybody in the house if you make such a clatter."

"What's that to me?" you say. "You have had your frolic. Now I've a mind to be merry myself," and you begin singing and shouting as loud as you can.

The woodman and his wife, being awakened by the noise, peep through a crack in the door. When they see a wolf is there, they are sadly frightened. The woodman runs for his axe and gives his wife a scythe.

"Do you stay behind," says the woodman, "and when I have knocked him on the head, you must rip him up with the scythe."

You hear all of this and cry out, "Father, Father! I am here. The wolf has swallowed me."

And your father says, "Heaven be praised! We have found our dear child again."

He tells his wife not to use the scythe for fear she should hurt you. Then he aims a great blow and strikes the wolf on the head and kills him on the spot! When he is dead, they cut open his body and set you free.

"What fears we have had for you!" says your father.

"Yes, Father," you answer, "I have traveled all over the world, I think, since we parted. Now I am very glad to come home and get fresh air again."

"Why, where have you been?" says your father.

"I have been in a mouse-hole and in a snail-shell and down a cow's throat and in the wolf's belly. Yet here I am again, safe and sound."

"Well," your parents say, "you are come back, and we will not sell you again for all the riches in the world."

Then they hug and kiss you and give you plenty to eat and drink, for you are very hungry. Then they fetch new clothes for you, for your old ones have been quite spoiled on your journey.

So you stay at home with your father and mother, in peace. For though you have been so great a traveler and have done and seen so many fine things and are fond enough of telling the whole story, you always agree that, after all, there's no place like home!

GO TO PAGE 51.

You comfort her and say, "Just wait a little, until the moon has risen, and then we will soon find the way."

And when the full moon has risen, you take your little sister by the hand and follow the pebbles, which shine like newly coined silver pieces and show you the way. You walk the whole night long and by break of day come once more to your father's house.

You knock at the door.

When the woman opens it and sees you, she says, "You naughty children! Why have you slept so long in the forest? We thought you were never coming back!"

The father, however, rejoices, for it had cut him to the heart to leave you two behind alone.

GO TO THE NEXT PAGE.

Not long afterwards, there is once more great dearth throughout the land, and you hear your mother saying at night to your father, "Everything is eaten again. We have one half loaf left, and that is the end. The children must go. We will take them farther into the wood, so they will not find their way out again. There is no other means of saving ourselves!"

The man's heart is heavy, and he says, "It would be better to share the last mouthful with the children."

The woman, however, will listen to nothing that he says, but she scolds and reproaches him. As he had yielded the first time, he has to do so a second time also.

When the old folks are asleep, you again get up and want to go out and pick up pebbles as you had done before. But the woman has locked the door, and you cannot get out.

Nevertheless, you comfort your sister and say, "Do not cry. Go to sleep quietly. The good God will help us."

* * *

Early in the morning, the woman comes and takes you and your sister out of your beds. A piece of bread is given to each of you, but it is smaller than the time

27

before. On the way into the forest, you crumble your bread in your pocket and often stand still to throw a morsel on the ground.

"Hansel, why do you stop and look around?" says your father. "Go on."

"I am looking back at my little pigeon, which is sitting on the roof and wants to say goodbye," you answer.

"Fool!" says the woman. "That is not your pigeon. That is the morning sun, shining on the chimney."

You, however, little by little, throw all the crumbs on the path.

The woman leads you still deeper into the forest, where you have never in your lives been before. Then a great fire is again made.

The mother says, "Just sit there, you children, and when you are tired you may sleep a little. We are going into the forest to cut wood. In the evening, when we are done, we will come and fetch you away."

When it is noon, Gretel shares her piece of bread with you, since you scattered yours along the way. Then you both fall asleep. Evening passes, but no one comes to you. You do not wake until it is dark night.

You comfort your little sister and say, "Just wait, Gretel, until the moon rises, and then we shall see the crumbs of bread, which I have strewn about. They will show us our way home again."

When the moon comes, you set out, but you find no crumbs—for the many thousands of birds which fly about in the woods and fields have picked them all up.

You say to Gretel, "We shall soon find the way," but you do not find it.

You look up to see the North Star, shining brightly to your right. You pause to wonder if you are going in the correct direction. Should you continue walking straight ahead, or are you better off turning around and going back the way you came?

Continue straight.

GO TO PAGE 47.

Turn around.

GO TO PAGE 52.

You remain locked in the stable, day after day and night after night. Those nights are cold, and you sleep poorly. You long to spend time with your sister. Yet you are only allowed to glimpse her briefly, each time she brings you water to drink or a meal to eat.

The food is the only good thing about this place. You eat the tastiest dishes and the sweetest treats. You know this is only because the witch is preparing you to her tastes—yet you eat her food all the same.

* * *

At the end of four weeks, the witch grows tired of waiting. When the water is boiling and the oven is warm, she comes to the stable and seizes you from your prison. She is surprised by how plump you've become, yet she is strong enough to drag you along.

There is no escape for you now. You are soon to be cooked like a goose. You only hope that fortune is kinder to your dear sister, Gretel.

GO TO PAGE 75.

You are a princess, and it is your 15th birthday. You have been cursed by an angry fairy: You will be wounded by a spindle and die within the next year. However, a kind fairy has softened the evil magic so that you will not die but shall instead sleep for 100 years.

As you wander the palace, alone, you come to a narrow staircase that leads to an old tower.

GO TO THE NEXT PAGE.

You follow the narrow staircase up toward the top of the tower. It ends with a little door, and in the door, there is a **GOLDEN KEY**.

When you turn it, the door springs open. You press the golden key into your pocket and step through the doorway. There sits an old lady spinning away busily.

"Why, how now, good mother," you say. "What are you doing there?"

"Spinning," says the old lady. She nods her head, humming a tune, while *buzz* goes the wheel.

"How prettily that little thing turns round!" you say.

The old lady invites you to join her, so you take the spindle and begin to try and spin.

Scarcely have you touched the spindle before the fairy's prophecy is fulfilled. The spindle wounds you, and you fall down lifeless on the ground. However, you are not dead but have only fallen into a deep sleep.

The king and the queen, who have just come home, and all their court, fall asleep. And the horses sleep in the stables and the dogs in the court, the pigeons on the house-top and the very flies upon the walls. Even the fire on the hearth stops blazing and goes to sleep. The jack stops, and the spit that was turning with a goose upon it for the king's dinner stands still. And the cook, who is at that moment pulling the kitchen-boy by the arm to give him a box on the ear for something he has done amiss, lets him go, and both fall asleep. The butler falls asleep with a jug of water at his lips—and, thus, everything stands still and sleeps soundly.

A large hedge of thorns soon grows around the palace, and every year it becomes higher and thicker.

At last, the old palace is surrounded and hidden so that not even the roof or the chimneys can be seen.

But there is a report through all the land of the beautiful sleeping Briar Rose (for so you are called). So, from time to time, several kings' sons come and try to break through the thicket into the palace.

This, however, none of them ever do, for the thorns and bushes lay hold of them, as if it were with hands. There, the young men stick fast and die wretchedly, all while you sleep.

WILL YOU USE THE GOLDEN KEY?

Yes.

GO TO PAGE 57.

No.

GO TO PAGE 75.

TOM THUMB

A poor woodman sits in his cottage one night, by the fireside, while his wife sits by his side, spinning thread with her spindle.

"How lovely it is, wife," he says, "for you and me to sit here, with our only child."

"What you say is very true," says the wife, turning her wheel. "How happy I knew I would always be if I had but one child! If it were ever so small—nay, if it were no bigger than my thumb—I should be very happy and love it dearly."

Odd as you may think it to be, it came to pass that this good woman's wish had been fulfilled, just in the very way she had wished it. For, not long afterwards, she had a little boy, who was quite healthy and strong but was not much bigger than a thumb.

So they had said, "Well, we cannot say we have not got what we wished for. Little as he is, we will still love him dearly."

You are their son, and they call you Tom Thumb.

They give you plenty of food, yet for all they do, you never grow bigger. You stay just the same size as you had been when you were born. Still, your eyes are sharp and sparkling, and you soon show yourself to be a clever little fellow.

One day, as the woodman gets ready to go into the forest to cut firewood, he says, "I wish I had someone to bring the cart after me, for I want to make haste."

"Oh, Father," you cry, "I will take care of that. The cart shall be in the wood by the time you want it."

Then the woodman laughs and says, "How can that be? You cannot reach up to the horse's bridle."

"Never mind that, Father," you say. "If my mother will only harness the horse, I will get into his ear and tell him which way to go."

When the time comes, the mother harnesses the horse to the cart and puts you into his ear. As you sit there, you tell the beast how to go, crying out, "Go on!" and "Stop!" as you want, and the horse goes on just as well as if the woodman had driven it himself.

It happens that, as the horse is going a little too fast and you are calling out, "Gently! gently!" two strangers come up.

"What an odd thing that is!" says one. "There is a cart going along, and I hear a carter talking to the horse, yet I can see no one."

"That is odd, indeed," says the other. "Let us follow the cart and see where it goes."

So they go on into the wood, till at last they come to the place where the woodman is.

Seeing your father, you cry out, "See, Father, here I am with the cart, all right and safe! Now take me down!"

So your father takes hold of the horse with one hand. With the other, he takes you out of the horse's ear and puts you down upon a straw, where you sit as merry as you please.

The two strangers are, all this time, looking on and do not know what to say for wonder.

At last, one takes the other aside and says, "That little urchin will make our fortune, if we can get him and carry him about from town to town as a show. We must buy him."

So they go up to the woodman and ask him what he will take for you.

"He will be better off," they say, "with us."

"I won't sell him at all," says your father. "My own flesh and blood is dearer to me than all the silver and gold in the world."

You consider this opportunity. Your parents are poor and could use the money—and this could be the start of your grand adventure. Or it could lead to your demise. You don't know these men. Should you go with them, or will you stay with your family?

Go.

GO TO PAGE 10.

Stay.

GO TO PAGE 45.

You leave a light burning and hide yourselves in a corner of the room, behind a curtain that is hung up there, and watch what will happen.

As soon as it is midnight, there comes in two little naked dwarfs. They sit themselves upon your bench, take up all the work that has been cut out, and begin to ply with their little fingers, stitching and rapping and tapping away at such a rate, that you are all wonder and cannot take your eyes off them.

And on they go, till the job is quite done, and the shoes stand ready for use upon the table. This is long before daybreak, and then they bustle away as quick as lightning.

* * *

The next day your wife says to you, "These little friends have made us rich, and we ought to be thankful to them and do them a good turn if we can. I am quite sorry to see them run about as they do, and indeed it is not very decent, for they have nothing upon their backs to keep off the cold. I'll tell you what: I will make each of them a shirt and a coat and a waistcoat and a pair of pantaloons into the bargain. You make each of them a little pair of shoes."

The thought pleases you very much.

* * *

One evening, when all the things are ready, you lay them on the table, instead of the work that you usually cut out. You go and hide yourselves, to watch what the little elves will do.

About midnight, in they come, dancing and skipping, hopping around the room. They go to sit down to their work, as usual—but when they see the clothes lying for them, they laugh and chuckle and seem mightily delighted.

Then they dress themselves in the twinkling of an eye and dance and caper and spring about, as merry as can be, till at last they dance out the door and away over the green.

You and your wife see them no more. But everything goes well with you from that time forward.

GO TO PAGE 51.

In the evening, you come to a little cottage and go in there to rest, for your weary feet will carry you no farther. Everything is spruce and neat in the cottage. A white cloth is spread on the table, and there are seven little plates with seven little loaves and seven little glasses and knives and forks laid in order. By the wall stand seven little beds.

Since you are exceedingly hungry, you pick a little piece off each loaf. After that, you decide to lie down and rest. So you try all the little beds. One is too long, and another is too short, till, at last, the seventh bed suits you. Lying there, you go to sleep.

* * *

You are still half asleep when you open your eyes, and you feel that you must be dreaming. You see seven little dwarfs enter the cottage. They look as if they live among the mountains, digging and searching for gold.

They light up their seven lamps and see directly that all is not right.

The first says, "Who has been sitting on my stool?"

The second says, "Who has been eating off my plate?"

The third says, "Who has been picking at my bread?"

The fourth says, "Who has been using my spoon?"

The fifth says, "Who has been handling my fork?"

The sixth says, "Who has been cutting with my knife?"

The seventh says, "Who has been drinking my milk?"

Then the first looks around and says, "Who has been lying on my bed?"

The rest come running to him, and everyone cries out that somebody has been upon his bed. But the seventh sees you and calls upon his brethren to come and look at you.

They cry out with wonder and astonishment. They bring their lamps, and gazing upon you, they say, "Good heavens! What a lovely child she is!"

They are delighted to see you, and they take care not to wake you further. So you sleep till the night is gone.

* * *

In the morning, you tell them all your story. They pity you and say that you stay where you are, and they will take good care of you. But they warn you, saying, "The queen will soon find out where you are, so take care and let no one in." Then they go out all day long to their work, seeking for gold and silver in the mountains.

You imagine the queen, now that she thinks you are dead, believing that she is certainly the handsomest lady in the land. You think of her going to her glass and saying,

"Tell me, glass, tell me true!
Of all the ladies in the land,
Who is fairest? tell me who?"

The glass will answer—

"Thou, Queen, thou are fairest in all this land.
But over the Hills, in the greenwood shade,
Where the seven dwarfs their dwelling have made,
There Snow-White is hiding; and she
Is lovelier far, O Queen, than thee."

Then the queen will be very much alarmed, for she knows that the glass always speaks the truth. She will be sure that the servant has betrayed her.

Your daydream is interrupted by a knock at the door and a voice that cries, "Fine wares to sell!"

You look out the window and say, "Good day, good woman. What have you to sell?"

"Good wares, fine wares," she replies. "Laces and bobbins of all colors, and beautiful combs too."

"I will let the old peddler woman in," you decide. "She seems to be a very good sort of person." You run down and unbolt the door.

"Bless me," says the woman, "what shall I give ye: laces or a comb?"

Take the laces.

GO TO PAGE 90.

Take a comb.

GO TO PAGE 56.

You follow the staircase down and down and down. For a time, you wonder if the stairs will ever end, and you wonder whether you should turn and go back.

The moment you decide to do so, you spy a sliver of light just ahead. As you continue downward, you see not one source of light but two, which come from behind two doorways.

The door to the left is tall and narrow, so much so that you will have to turn sideways to squeeze through. The door to the right is short and wide. To get through, you will have to crawl on your hands and knees. Above it, a sign warns, "No golden objects allowed through this door." Should you try one of these doorways, or will you go to the top of the tower?

Go left.

GO TO PAGE 20.

Go up.

GO TO PAGE 32.

Go right.

GO TO PAGE 34.

"My father won't sell me," you tell the strangers, "and I won't go with you."

"We tried to do this honest and fair," says one of the men. "But you're the key to our fortune. If you won't come willingly, we'll just have to take you!"

The two men lunge forward before your father can react. One of them grabs his axe before it can be swung. The other tackles your father to the ground.

As they wrestle, the men roll toward you, putting you in grave danger. You leap from your place and run for your life. You narrowly avoid getting squished by the tangle of men.

However, the commotion has startled the horse. It begins to neigh and kick and buck. Too late, you realize that your path away from the men has led you too close to the horse.

For a moment, you find yourself standing in the shadow of something large. You look up to glimpse a giant, thick, powerful hoof crashing down toward you.

It is the last sight you ever see.

GO TO PAGE 75.

Although you are greatly fearful, you swallow loudly and say, "I cannot make such a deal."

The enchantress grins wickedly. "Very well," she says. "You steal from me like a wolf." She raises her arms as if to cast a spell. "Therefore, a wolf you shall become!"

She waves and flicks her hands in a peculiar motion, and then there is a flash of purple light.

GO TO PAGE 74.

You comfort her and say, "Yes, let us go, and we will soon find the way."

The full moon has not yet risen, so the path is dark and hard to see. Yet you continue forward. You walk the whole night long and by break of day come to a cottage. You are surprised to find its door standing open.

When you go inside, you call out, "Help us, for we are two lost children!"

When you receive no answer, you go to the bedroom.

There lies an old woman with her cap pulled far over her face and looking very strange.

"Hello," you say, "we mean you no harm. We are but two lost children."

There is no reply.

You step closer, to make certain the old woman is feeling okay.

With one bound, the wolf is out of bed, and he reveals his disguise. "I was expecting someone else, but you will do well for my next meal! I put on this woman's clothes, dressed in her cap, laid in bed, and drew the curtains."

And scarcely has the wolf said this, than he has swallowed you up.

GO TO PAGE 75.

47

The door is big enough to fit through, and the flames are hot enough to roast you. Yet you know the witch will not cook you. She hasn't bothered to make you plump yet. So you creep up and thrust your head into the oven. Then you quickly back away.

"Now, now," snaps the witch. "You barely checked it at all. Do as I say!"

You creep up again and lean farther into the oven. At that moment, the witch gives you a push that drives you far into it. She shuts the iron door and fastens the bolt.

There is no escape. You are soon to be cooked like a goose. You only hope that fortune is kinder to your dear brother, Hansel.

GO TO PAGE 75.

"Yes, I agree," you tell him.

So your little friend takes the ring and begins to work at the wheel again, and he whistles and sings:

> "Round about, round about,
> Lo and behold!
> Reel away, reel away,
> Straw into gold!"

Before the sun rises, all is done once more.

The king is happy to see his riches. He promises to keep his word and marry you. But he never gets the chance, for you are again visited by Allerleirauh.

"I warned you that we needed the golden ring," she says, "but you have given it away. Now, we shall never find it again. All hope is lost."

Even though it is still midday, a dreadful darkness spreads across the land—across all lands. You watch helplessly as this world, this reality, crumbles and fades away, until all that is left is nothing.

GO TO PAGE 75.

You pocket a strand of **GOLDEN HAIR** and escape quickly from the tower. You roam about in misery.

At length, you come to a desert. You hear a voice, and it seems so familiar that you go toward it. When you approach, you are surprised to discover Rapunzel. She falls on your neck and weeps.

She tells you, "The enchantress knew nothing of our plan, until once I said to her, 'Tell me, Dame Gothel, how it happens that you are so much heavier for me to draw up than my father.'

"'Ah! You wicked child,' cried the enchantress. 'What do I hear you say? I thought I had separated you from all the world, and yet you have deceived me!'

"In anger, she clutched my beautiful tresses, wrapped them twice around her left hand, seized a pair of scissors with her right, and snip-snap, my lovely braids were cut off. And she was so pitiless that she took me into this desert, where I stayed in great grief and misery."

You lead your daughter home, where Rapunzel is joyfully received, and you live for a long time afterwards, happy and contented.

GO TO THE NEXT PAGE.

Yet one night you awaken to a familiar glow. It is Allerleirauh.

"You have done well so far, young one. But there is much yet to do. Tell me," she says, "have you yet found the **GOLDEN KEY**?"

IF YOUR ANSWER IS "NO," GO TO PAGE 31.

Next, she asks, "Do you have the **GOLDEN DUST**?"

IF YOUR ANSWER IS "NO," GO TO PAGE 34.

"What about the **GOLDEN HAIR?**" she says.

IF YOUR ANSWER IS "NO," GO TO PAGE 20.

"And have you discovered the **GOLDEN RING**?" she asks at last.

IF YOUR ANSWER IS "NO," GO TO PAGE 81.

You walk the whole night and all the next day, too, from morning till evening, but you do not get out of the forest. You are very hungry, for you have had nothing to eat. As you are both so weary that your legs will carry you no longer, you and Gretel lie down beneath a tree and fall asleep.

GO TO THE NEXT PAGE.

It is now three mornings since you left your father's house. You begin to walk again, but you always come deeper into the forest. If help does not come soon, you shall die of hunger and weariness.

When it is midday, you see a beautiful snow-white bird sitting on a bough, and it sings so delightfully that you stand still and listen to it. And when its song is over, it spreads its wings and flies away. You follow it until you reach a little house, on the roof of which the bird settles.

When you approach the little house, you see that it is built of bread and covered with cakes, but the windows are of clear sugar.

"We will set to work on that," you say, "and have a good meal. I will eat a bit of the roof. You, Gretel, can eat some of the window. It will taste sweet."

You reach up above and break off a little of the roof to try how it tastes. Gretel leans against the window and nibbles at the panes.

Then a soft voice cries from the parlor:

"Nibble, nibble, gnaw,
Who is nibbling at my little house?"

You answer,

"The wind, the wind,
The heaven-born wind."

You like the taste of the roof, so you tear down a great piece of it. Gretel pushes out the whole of a round window-pane, sits down, and enjoys herself with it.

Suddenly the door opens. A woman as old as the hills, who supports herself on crutches, comes creeping out. You and Gretel are so terribly frightened that you let fall what you had in your hands.

The old woman, however, nods her head and says, "You dear children, who has brought you here? Do come in, and stay with me. No harm shall happen to you."

She takes you both by the hand and leads you into her little house. Good food is set before you: milk and pancakes with sugar, apples, and nuts.

Afterwards, two pretty little beds are covered with clean white linen. You and Gretel lie down in them and think you are in heaven.

Yet, early the next morning, you are awakened when the old woman seizes you with her shriveled hand. She carries you into a little stable and drops you.

"I only pretended to be so kind," she says. "I am, in reality, a wicked witch, who lies in wait for children.

I only built the little house of bread in order to entice them here. When a child falls into my power, I cook and eat it. Witches have red eyes and cannot see far, but we have a keen scent like the beasts and are aware when human beings draw near. When you came into my neighborhood, I laughed with malice and said, 'I have them. They shall not escape me again!' When I saw both of you looking so pretty, with your plump and rosy cheeks, I said to myself, 'That will be a dainty mouthful!'" Then she locks you in behind a grated door.

Scream as you might, it does not help. You watch as the wicked witch goes inside, and you listen as she shouts at Gretel.

You cannot escape on your own. You need the aid of magic. Perhaps one of your golden items can get you out of this place.

Yes.

GO TO PAGE 60.

No.

GO TO PAGE 30.

You say to the woman, "Oh, look at the beautiful combs. I would like to have one."

She gives you a comb, and it looks so pretty that you take it up and put it into your hair to try it. But the moment it touches your head, the poison is so powerful that you fall down senseless.

"There you may lie," says the queen, and she goes on her way.

When the dwarfs return that evening, they see you lying on the ground. No breath passes your lips, and they realize with dread that you are quite dead.

GO TO PAGE 75.

When you open your eyes, you are a shoemaker, who works very hard and is very honest. But still you cannot earn enough to live upon. At last, all you have in the world is gone, save just leather enough to make one pair of shoes.

You cut your leather out, all ready to make into shoes the next day, meaning to rise early in the morning to your work. Your conscience is clear and your heart light amidst all your troubles. So you go peaceably to bed, leaving all your cares to Heaven.

* * *

In the morning, after you have said your prayers, you sit yourself down to your work. To your great wonder, there stand the shoes, already made, upon the table. You know not what to say or think at such an odd thing happening. You look at the workmanship; there is not one false stitch in the whole job. All is so neat and true that it is quite a masterpiece.

The same day, a customer comes in, and the shoes suit him so well that he willingly pays a price higher than usual for them. With the money, you buy leather enough to make two pairs more.

In the evening, you cut out the work and go to bed early, so you might get up and begin in good time the next day. But you are saved all the trouble; for when you get up in the morning, the work is done as if by your own hand.

Soon, in come buyers, who pay you handsomely for your goods. So you buy leather enough for four pairs more. You cut out the work again overnight and find it done in the morning, as before.

And so it goes on for some time: What is got ready in the evening is always done by daybreak, and you soon are thriving and well-off again.

GO TO THE NEXT PAGE.

One evening, about Christmastime, you and your wife are sitting beside the fire, chatting together.

You say to her, "I should like to sit up and watch tonight, so we may see who it is that comes and does my work for me."

The wife likes the thought—so will you hide inside a closet or behind a curtain?

Hide in a closet.

GO TO PAGE 16.

Hide behind a curtain.

GO TO PAGE 38.

You clutch the golden hair and speak your wish. "Let me be free from here."

The air around you begins to swirl. It grows brighter and brighter. You press your eyes closed and cover your ears, until at last everything is still.

When you open your eyes, you are no longer in the stable. You are inside the little house that is built of bread and covered with cakes. You are in a bed covered with clean white linens. And you are now Gretel.

"Get up, lazy thing. Fetch some water, and cook something good for your brother. He is in the stable and is to be made fat. When he is fat, I will eat him."

You begin to weep bitterly, but it is all in vain, for you are forced to do what the wicked witch commands.

And now the best food is cooked for Hansel, but you get nothing but crab-shells.

* * *

Every morning, the woman creeps to the little stable and cries, "Hansel, stretch out your finger that I may feel if you will soon be fat."

Hansel, however, stretches out a little chicken bone to her. The old woman, who has dim eyes, cannot see it and thinks it is his finger. She is astonished that there is no way of fattening him.

* * *

When four weeks have gone by and he still remains thin, she is seized with impatience and will not wait any longer. "Now then, Gretel," she cries to you, "stir yourself, and bring some water. Let Hansel be fat or lean. Tomorrow I will kill him and cook him."

Ah, how you do lament when you have to fetch the water and how your tears do flow down your cheeks!

"Dear God, do help us," you cry. "If the wild beasts in the forest had but devoured us, we should at any rate have died together."

"Just keep your noise to yourself," says the old woman. "It won't help you at all."

* * *

Early in the morning, you have to go out and hang up the cauldron with the water and light the fire.

"We will bake first," says the old woman. "I have already heated the oven and kneaded the dough." She pushes you out to the oven, from which flames of fire are already darting. "Creep in," says the witch, "and see if it is properly heated so that we can put the bread in."

Is this a trick? Does she mean to cook you too? If you obey her, you must trust that she won't cook you . . . yet. If you refuse, you will certainly face her wrath—but you will not be cooked.

Get in.

GO TO PAGE 48.

Do not get in.

GO TO PAGE 104.

BRIAR ROSE

You pick up the rose and are momentarily blinded by a bright-white light. You shield your eyes with your arm and squeeze them closed. When you open your eyes, you are in another realm. The woman is gone.

This realm's king and queen have plenty of money and plenty of fine clothes to wear and plenty of good things to eat and drink and a coach to ride in every day. But although they have been married many years, they have no children. This grieves them very much.

As you walk by a river, at the bottom of a garden, you spy the queen. At the same moment, she sees a poor little fish that has thrown itself out of the water and lies gasping and nearly dead on the bank.

The queen takes pity on the little fish and throws it back into the river.

Before it swims away, it lifts its head out of the water and says, "I know what your wish is, and it shall be fulfilled, in return for your kindness to me. You will soon have a daughter."

As the fish swims away, you run past the queen, never taking your eyes off the magical creature; you dare not lose sight of it. Along the riverbank, you come upon an old fishing pole. You cast its line into the river, ahead of the fish. Your float is dragged away, deep into the water. In reeling it up, you pull out the magical fish.

"Let me live!" the fish exclaims. "If you release me, I shall grant you a wish."

You unhook the fish and drop it into the river.

It lifts its head out of the water. "Thank you, kind friend. I know you long for a better life—for wealth and adventure. I can grant you one but not both. Now, what is your wish?"

GO TO THE NEXT PAGE.

If you ask for wealth, you will have good food and fine clothes and a wonderful place to live. If you ask for adventure, you will remain poor, but your life shall be changed in unexpected ways.

Wish for wealth.

GO TO PAGE 17.

Wish for adventure.

GO TO PAGE 34.

You ascend the tower—but instead of finding your dear Rapunzel, you find the enchantress. She has fastened the braids of Rapunzel's hair, which she must have cut off, to the hook of the window.

The enchantress gazes at you with wicked and venomous looks. "Aha!" she cries mockingly. "You would fetch your dear daughter, but the beautiful bird sits no longer singing in the nest. The cat has got it and will scratch out your eyes, as well. Rapunzel is lost to you. You will never see her again."

You are beside yourself with pain. In your despair, you leap down from the tower. You escape with your life, but the thorns into which you fall pierce your eyes.

You spend the rest of your days wandering quite blind about the forest, eating nothing but roots and berries, and doing nothing but lamenting and weeping over the loss of your dear daughter.

GO TO PAGE 75.

You are surprised to find the cottage-door standing open. When you go into the room, you have such a strange feeling that you say to yourself, "Oh dear! How uneasy I feel today, and at other times I like being with my grandmother so much."

You call out, "Good morning," but receive no answer. So you go to the bed and draw back the curtains. There lies your grandmother with her cap pulled far over her face and looking very strange.

"Grandmother," you say, "what big ears you have!"

"The better to hear you with, my child," is the reply.

"But Grandmother, what big eyes you have!" you say.

"The better to see you with, my dear."

"But Grandmother, what large hands you have!"

"The better to hug you with."

"Oh, but, Grandmother, what a terrible big mouth you have!"

"The better to eat you with!"

With one bound, the wolf is out of bed, and he reveals his disguise. "I ran straight to your grandmother's house and knocked at the door. Pretending to be you, I lifted the latch. The door sprang open, and without saying a word, I went straight to your grandmother's bed and devoured her. Then I put on her clothes, dressed in her cap, laid in bed, and drew the curtains."

And scarcely has the wolf said this, than with one bound he is out of bed and has swallowed you up.

Yes.

GO TO PAGE 120.

No.

GO TO PAGE 75.

In your terror, you consent to everything!

* * *

Less than a year later, your wife is brought to bed, where she gives birth to a baby girl. The enchantress appears at once, gives the child the name of Rapunzel, and takes the child away with her.

GO TO THE NEXT PAGE.

Over the years, you hear tales of your daughter, Rapunzel. She grows into the most beautiful child under the sun. Yet when she is 12 years old, the enchantress shuts her into a tower, hidden in a forest. The tower has neither stairs nor door, but at the top is a little window.

When the enchantress wants to go in, she places herself beneath it and cries:

"Rapunzel, Rapunzel,
Let down your hair to me."

Rapunzel has magnificent long hair, fine as spun gold. When she hears the voice of the enchantress, she unfastens her braided tresses, winds them around one of the hooks of the window above, and then her **GOLDEN HAIR** falls 75 feet down, and the enchantress climbs up by it.

You cannot imagine these stories to be true.

GO TO THE NEXT PAGE.

After a year or two, it comes to happen that you ride through the forest and pass by a tower. You hear a song, which is so charming that you stand still and listen. You want to climb up, and you look for the door of the tower, but none is to be found.

You ride home, but the singing has so deeply touched your heart that every day you go out into the forest and listen to it.

Once, when you are standing behind a tree, you see the enchantress come there, and you hear how she cries:

> "Rapunzel, Rapunzel,
> Let down your hair to me."

Rapunzel lets down her hair, and the enchantress climbs up to her.

"If that is the ladder by which one climbs, I, too, will try," you say.

The next day, when it begins to grow dark, you go to the tower and cry:

> "Rapunzel, Rapunzel,
> Let down your hair to me."

Immediately, the hair falls down and you climb up.

At first, Rapunzel is terribly frightened when you come to her, but you begin to talk to her quite like her father. Then Rapunzel loses her fear.

When you ask if she will return home with you, she says, "I will willingly go away with you, but I do not know how to get down. Bring with you a skein of silk every time that you come, and I will weave a ladder with it. When that is ready, I will descend, and you will take me home on your horse."

You agree that, until that time, you will come to her every evening, for the enchantress comes by day.

* * *

Many months pass, and each evening, Rapunzel lets down her hair for you immediately upon your arrival. Yet, one evening, you must call to her:

"Rapunzel, Rapunzel,
Let down your hair to me."

You shout to her three times before she lets down her hair. This gives you pause, and you sense trouble. Should you climb up to investigate? Or will you ride away from this tower and escape whatever danger awaits?

Climb up.

GO TO PAGE 66.

Escape.

GO TO PAGE 50.

You are a wolf with a wicked look in your eyes. You prowl twice or thrice around the house of Little Red-Cap's grandmother, waiting for them to open the door so you can eat them up.

At last, you jump on the roof, intending to wait until Red-Cap goes home in the evening. Then you can steal after her and devour her in the darkness.

In front of the house is a great stone trough, and you hear the grandmother say, "Take the pail, Red-Cap. I made some sausages yesterday, so carry the water in which I boiled them to the trough."

Red-Cap carries and pours until the great trough is quite full. Then the smell of the sausages reaches you, and you sniff and peep down and at last stretch out your neck so far that you can no longer keep your footing. You begin to slip and slip down from the roof straight into the great trough—and are drowned.

GO TO THE NEXT PAGE.

THE END

TRY AGAIN

This matter is too important to trust to anyone else. You must venture out and find the answer for yourself. It is the only hope to save your poor child.

As hurry through the wood, you say to yourself, "I must take care not to go near to the evil fairy's castle."

It is a beautiful morning. The first rays of the rising sun shine brightly through the long stems of the trees upon the green underwood beneath.

You wander a long way. When you look to see which way you should go next, you find yourself at a loss to know what path to take. You look behind you and see through the bushes that you have, without knowing it, walked close under the old walls of the castle. Then you shrink for fear, turn pale, and tremble.

To calm yourself, you start to sing, but your song stops suddenly. You have been changed into a nightingale, and your song ends with a mournful *jug, jug.*

The old fairy comes forth, pale and meager, with staring eyes and a nose and chin that almost meet one another. She seizes you and goes away with you in her hand. She cackles and says, "I will keep you and cage you, and you will sing to me for the rest of your days."

GO TO PAGE 75.

You run from the path into the wood to look for flowers. And whenever you pick one, you fancy that you see a still prettier one farther on and run after it—and so you go deeper and deeper into the wood. You even find a **GOLDEN FLOWER**.

When you have gathered so many flowers that you can carry no more, you remember your grandmother and set out on the way to her.

GO TO THE NEXT PAGE.

You are surprised to find the cottage-door standing open. When you go into the room, you have such a strange feeling that you say to yourself, "Oh dear! How uneasy I feel today, and at other times I like being with my grandmother so much."

You call out, "Good morning," but receive no answer. So you go to the bed and draw back the curtains. There lies your grandmother with her cap pulled far over her face and looking very strange.

"Grandmother," you say, "what big ears you have!"

"The better to hear you with, my child," is the reply.

"But Grandmother, what big eyes you have!" you say.

"The better to see you with, my dear."

"But Grandmother, what large hands you have!"

"The better to hug you with."

"Oh, but, Grandmother, what a terrible big mouth you have!"

"The better to eat you with!"

With one bound, the wolf is out of bed, and he reveals his disguise. "I ran straight to your grandmother's house and knocked at the door. Pretending to be you, I lifted the latch. The door sprang open, and without saying a word, I went straight to your grandmother's bed and devoured her. Then I put on her clothes, dressed in her cap, laid in bed, and drew the curtains."

And scarcely has the wolf said this, than with one bound he is out of bed and has swallowed you up.

Yes.

GO TO PAGE 120.

No.

GO TO PAGE 75.

You shake your head. "I will make no such deal with you, frog. I shall get the golden ball myself, for perhaps I can reach it."

"Very well," says the frog, "best of luck. Do be careful, as the water is deep. And watch out for the duck."

The duck, you think, *what a silly thing to say.*

When the frog is safely out of sight, you lie down by the pond and stretch toward the ball. The water is deep, as the frog had said, and the ball remains out of reach. So you inch forward and try for it again. You do hope not to get your dress wet, but the ball remains too distant from you.

At that moment, out of meanness, the duck swims quickly to you, seizes your head in its beak and draws you into the water, and there you sadly drown.

GO TO PAGE 75.

LITTLE SNOW-WHITE

You are a young girl, about seven years old. Your skin is as white as snow, your cheeks as rosy as blood, and your hair as black as ebony. You are called Snow-White.

You are led away from your father's castle, deep into the forest, by a servant. But you do not understand why.

"Your mother, the queen, died. Your father, the king, has married another wife," the servant tells you. "She is very beautiful but so proud that she cannot bear to think that anyone could surpass her. She has a magical looking-glass, to which she gazes upon herself and says,

'Tell me, glass, tell me true!
Of all the ladies in the land,
Who is fairest? Tell me who?'

"The glass has always answered, 'Thou, Queen, art fairest in the land.'

"But you have grown more and more beautiful," says the servant. "You are as bright as the day and fairer than the queen herself. Today, the glass answered the queen, when she went to consult it as usual—

'Thou, Queen, may'st fair and beauteous be,
But Snow-White is lovelier far than thee?'

"When the queen heard this, she turned pale with rage and envy. She said to me, 'Take Snow-White away into the wide wood, that I may never see her more.'"

"Please, spare my life," you cry.

The servant's expression softens, as if his heart has melted. He says, "I will not hurt you, but it is most likely that wild beasts will tear you to pieces."

So he leaves you there, to face your fate alone.

GO TO THE NEXT PAGE.

You wander along through the wood in great fear. The wild beasts roar around, but none do you any harm. Then you notice pretty flowers growing everywhere. Will you stop and pick them? They may brighten your sour mood. Or shall you continue wandering through the wood?

Pick flowers.

GO TO PAGE 9.

Continue onward.

GO TO PAGE 40.

You dance till a late hour of the night.

When you tire and want to go home, the king's son says, "I shall go and take you to your home," for he wants to see where you live.

But you slip away from him and run off towards home. The prince follows, so you jump up into the pigeon-house and shut the door. So he waits till your father comes home and tells him that you who had been at the feast have hidden yourself in the pigeon-house.

But when they break open the door, they find no one within. And as they come back into the house, you lie, as you always do, in your dirty frock by the ashes—for you had run as quickly as you could through the pigeon-house and onto the hazel-tree and had there taken off your beautiful clothes and laid them beneath the tree, so the birds might carry them away. Then you had seated yourself amid the ashes again in your little old frock.

* * *

The next day—when the feast is again held and your father, mother, and sisters are gone—you go to the hazel-tree. All happens as the evening before.

The king's son, who has been waiting for you, takes you by the hand and dances with you.

When anyone asks you to dance, he says as before, "This lady is dancing with me."

When night comes and you want to go home, the king's son goes with you. But you spring away from him all at once into the garden behind your father's house.

In this garden stands a fine, large pear-tree. You jump up into it without being seen.

Then the king's son waits till your father comes home and says to him, "The unknown lady has slipped away, and I think she must have sprung into the pear-tree."

The father orders an axe to be brought and prepares to chop down the tree. Should you allow him to do this, or will you stop him from cutting down the pear-tree?

Remain hidden.

GO TO PAGE 124.

Stop your father.

GO TO PAGE 102.

"You are kind, frog," you say, "to release me from our bargain. I shall accept your offer, and you may keep the golden ball."

The frog croaks bitterly. His eyes become wet. His face wears a heartbroken expression. Yet he says nothing further. He simply takes the ball in his mouth, turns away from you, and begins his long journey back toward the pond.

You feel saddened at first, but those emotions are soon replaced by a sense of relief. The frog is out of your life, and you are free from this burden.

GO TO PAGE 137.

You are a prince, and you come and call on a house of dwarfs. Nearby, you find a coffin of glass placed upon a hill. The words "Snow-White, a king's daughter" are written on it in golden letters. A young woman rests peacefully inside and still only looks as though she is asleep, for she is even now as white as snow and as red as blood and as black as ebony.

A dwarf sits by the coffin, watching her. He says, "Some 10 years ago, we found Snow-White lying on the ground. No breath passed her lips, and we were afraid that she was quite dead. We lifted her up and combed her hair and washed her face, but all was in vain. So we laid her down upon a bier, and all seven of us watched and bewailed her three whole days.

"And then we proposed to bury her, but we would never bury her in the cold ground. We made a coffin of glass so that we might still look at her. One of us always sits by it and watches. And the birds of the air came, too, and bemoaned Snow-White. First of all came an owl, and then a raven, but at last came a dove."

All the dwarfs gather, and you offer them money and earnestly pray them to let you take her away.

But they say, "We will not part with her for all the gold in the world."

At last, however, they have pity on you and give you the coffin. But the moment you lift it up to carry it home with you, a piece of apple falls from between her lips.

Snow-White awakens and exclaims, "Where am I?"

And you answer, "Thou art safe with me." Then you tell her all that has happened and say, "I love you better than all the world. Come with me to my father's palace, and you shall be my wife."

Snow-White consents and goes home with you, and everything is prepared with great pomp and splendor for your wedding.

To the feast, you invite, among the rest, Snow-White's old enemy, the queen. As she is dressing herself in fine, rich clothes, she looks in the glass and says,

> "Tell me, glass, tell me true!
> Of all the ladies in the land,
> Who is fairest? Tell me who?"

And the glass answers,

> "Thou, lady, art the loveliest here, I ween;
> But lovelier far is the new-made queen."

When she hears this, the queen starts with rage. But her envy and curiosity are so great that she cannot help setting out to see the bride.

And when she arrives and sees that it is no other than Snow-White, whom she thought had been dead a long while, she chokes with passion and falls ill and dies.

But Snow-White and you live and reign happily over the land for many, many years.

GO TO PAGE 140.

"Bless me," says the woman, "how badly your stays are laced. Let me lace them up with one of my nice new laces."

You stand up before the old woman, who sets to work so nimbly and pulls the lace so tightly that you lose your breath and fall down as if you are dead.

"There's an end of all thy beauty," says the spiteful queen, and she goes away home.

GO TO THE NEXT PAGE.

In the evening, the seven dwarfs return, and how grieved they are to see you stretched upon the ground motionless, as if you are quite dead. However, they lift you up—and when they find what is the matter, they cut the lace.

In a little time, you begin to breathe and soon come to yourself again.

Then they say, "The old woman was the queen. Take care another time, and let no one in when we are away."

* * *

The next day, you imagine when the queen got home, she went to her glass and spoke to it—but to her surprise, it replied in the same words as before.

Again, your daydream is interrupted by a knock at the cottage door. It is a woman—but very different from the one who came before.

You put your head out of the window and say, "I dare not let anyone in, for the dwarfs have told me not to."

"Do as you please," says the old woman, "but at any rate, take this pretty apple. I will make you a present of it." She holds out a **GOLDEN APPLE** that looks very rosy and tempting."

"No," you say, "I dare not take it."

"You silly girl," answers the other. "What are you afraid of? Do you think it is poisoned? Come! You eat one part, and I will eat the other."

You are very much tempted to taste it, for the apple looks exceedingly nice. When you see the old woman eat, you can refrain no longer. But you have scarcely put the piece into your mouth when you fall down dead upon the ground.

"Ha! The apple is so prepared that one side is good, though the other side is poisoned. This time nothing will save thee," says the queen, and she returns home to her glass.

GO TO THE NEXT PAGE.

HANSEL AND GRETEL

By a great forest dwells a poor wood-cutter with his wife and his two children. You are their son, Hansel, and your sister is Gretel. When great dearth falls on the land, your family no longer has even daily bread to eat.

By night in your bed, you are not able to sleep for hunger. You overhear your father say to his wife, "What is to become of us? How are we to feed the poor children, when we no longer have anything even for ourselves?"

"I'll tell you what, husband," answers the woman. "Early tomorrow morning, we will take the children out into the forest to where it is the thickest. There, we will light a fire for them and give each of them one more piece of bread. Then we will go to our work and leave them alone. They will not find the way home again, and we shall be rid of them."

"No, wife," says the man, "I will not do that. How can I bear to leave my children alone in the forest? The wild animals would soon come and tear them to pieces."

"Oh, you fool!" says she. "Then we must all four die of hunger. You may as well plane the planks for our coffins," and she leaves him no peace until he agrees to her plan.

"But I feel very sorry for the poor children, all the same," says the man.

Gretel weeps bitter tears and says to you, "Now all is over with us."

"Be quiet, Gretel," you say, "Do not distress yourself. I will soon find a way to help us."

When the old folks have fallen asleep, you get up, put on your little coat, open the door below, and creep outside. The moon shines brightly, and the white pebbles in front of the house glitter like real silver pennies. You stoop and stuff the little pocket of your coat with as many pebbles as you can.

You go back and say to Gretel, "Be comforted, dear little sister, and sleep in peace. God will not forsake us."

GO TO THE NEXT PAGE.

When day dawns, the woman comes and wakes the two of you, saying, "Get up, you sluggards! We are going into the forest to fetch wood." She gives each of you a little piece of bread and says, "There is something for your dinner, but do not eat it up before then, for you will get nothing else."

Gretel puts the bread under her apron, since you have the pebbles in your pocket. Then you all set out together on the way to the forest.

When you have walked a short time, you stop and peep back at the house, and you do so again and again.

Your father says, "Hansel, what are you looking at there and staying behind for? Pay attention, and do not forget how to use your legs."

"Ah, Father," you say, "I am looking at my little white cat, which is sitting up on the roof and wants to say goodbye to me."

The wife says, "Fool, that is not your little cat. That is the morning sun, which is shining on the chimneys."

You, however, have not been looking back at the cat but have been constantly throwing one of the white pebble-stones out of your pocket on the road.

GO TO THE NEXT PAGE.

When you reach the middle of the forest, your father says, "Now, children, pile up some wood, and I will light a fire that you may not be cold."

You and your sister gather brushwood together, as high as a little hill. The brushwood is lighted.

When the flames burn very high, the woman says, "Now, children, lay yourselves down by the fire and rest. We will go into the forest and cut some wood. When we are done, we will come back and fetch you away."

You sit by the fire, and when noon comes, you eat a little piece of bread. Since you can hear the strokes of the wood-axe, you know that your father is still near. (It is not the axe, however, but a branch that has been fastened to a withered tree—which the wind blows backwards and forwards.)

After sitting such a long time, your eyes close with fatigue, and you fall fast asleep.

GO TO THE NEXT PAGE.

When at last you wake, it is already getting dark.

Gretel begins to cry and says, "How are we to get out of the forest now?"

You know how, but dusk is a dangerous time to walk through the wood—animals are on the hunt. Yet the longer you wait, the colder and darker it becomes.

Wait.

GO TO PAGE 26.

Leave now.

GO TO PAGE 47.

What nonsense, you think, *this silly frog is talking. He can never even get out of the pond to visit me, though he may be able to get my ball for me. Therefore, I will tell him he shall have what he asks.*

So you say to the frog, "Well, if you will bring me my ball, I will do all you ask."

Then the frog puts his head down and dives deep under the water. After a little while, he comes up again, with the ball in his mouth. He throws it on the edge of the pond.

As soon as you see your ball, you run to pick it up. You are so overjoyed to have it in your hand again that you never think of the frog, but you run home as fast as you can.

The frog calls after you, "Stay, princess, and take me with you as you said."

But you do not stop to hear a word.

* * *

The next day, just as you sit down to dinner, you hear a strange noise: *tap, tap—plash, plash.* It is as if something is coming up the marble staircase. Soon afterwards, there is a gentle knock at the door.

A little voice cries out and says:

"Open the door, my princess dear,
Open the door to thy true love here!
And mind the words that you and I said
By the fountain cool, in the greenwood shade."

You run to the door and open it, and there you see the frog, whom you had quite forgotten. At this sight, you are sadly frightened. Shutting the door as fast as you can, you come back to your seat.

The king, your father, seeing that something has frightened you, asks what is the matter.

"There is a nasty frog," you say, "at the door, that lifted my ball for me out of the pond this morning. I told him that he should live with me here, thinking that he could never get out of the pond—but there he is at the door, and he wants to come in."

The frog knocks again at the door and says:

"Open the door, my princess dear,
Open the door to thy true love here!
And mind the words that you and I said
By the fountain cool, in the greenwood shade."

Then the king says to you, "As you have given your word, you must keep it. So go and let him in."

You do so. The frog hops into the room and then straight on—*tap, tap—plash, plash*—from the bottom of the room to the top, till he comes up close to the table where you sit.

"Please lift me upon my chair," he says, "and let me sit next to you." As soon as you have done this, the frog says, "Put your plate nearer to me, so I may eat from it."

This you do.

When he has eaten as much as he can, he says, "Now I am tired. Carry me upstairs and put me into bed."

Although very unwilling, you take him up in your hand and put him upon the pillow of your own bed, where you sleep all night long.

As soon as it is light, he jumps up, hops downstairs, and goes out of the house.

Now, then, you think, *at last he is gone, and I shall be troubled with him no more.*

But you are mistaken, for when night comes again, you hear the same tapping at the door.

GO TO THE NEXT PAGE.

The frog comes once more and says:

"Open the door, my princess dear,
Open the door to thy true love here!
And mind the words that you and I said
By the fountain cool, in the greenwood shade."

When you open the door, the frog comes in and sleeps upon your pillow as before, till morning breaks.

And the third night, he returns again.

"I made you a promise," you say to the frog, "but won't you release me from it? Is there anything I can do to escape this torment?"

The frog sighs heavily but considers your question. "If you return to me the golden ball, I shall take it and go. You will never see me again."

Give away the ball.

GO TO PAGE 86.

Allow the frog to stay.

GO TO PAGE 136.

You lie in the kitchen, in the ashes, as usual; for you had slipped down on the other side of the tree and carried your beautiful clothes back to the bird at the hazel-tree, and then put on your little old frock.

Yet when you see your father about to cut down his pear-tree, you decide that you must stop him. So you leap to your feet and hurry out the door.

"Father, stop," you cry. "Here I am!"

Your arrival is ill-timed. Not only are you too late to save the pear-tree, but the tree falls down on your head and kills you on the spot.

GO TO PAGE 75.

"I ask for a golden necklace, dear father, that I can wear and feel pretty," you say.

He departs, intent on buying the gifts that each of his daughters requested. Yet he does not return home. As worry for him mounts, you begin to wonder what might have happened to him.

The answer arrives in the form of a messenger. "Your father purchased an expensive golden necklace," says he. "Then he was followed by two men. They had failed to rob the parson's house, so they mugged your father instead. I'm sorry to say he was injured in the skirmish and has passed away."

News of his death sends a shock through your body. You go to your mother's grave and weep. Your father died because of the gift for which you asked.

It isn't enough that you blame yourself. Your stepmother blames you, as well. She allows you to keep the clothes on your back and nothing more, as she casts you out of the home forever.

You are alone with nowhere to live and nowhere to go. As you escape into the forest, you wonder with dread what horrible fate awaits you.

GO TO PAGE 75.

You say, "I do not know how I am to do it. How do I get in?"

"Silly goose," says the old woman. "The door is big enough. Just look; I can get in myself!" She creeps up and thrusts her head into the oven.

Then you give her a push that drives her far into it and shut the iron door and fasten the bolt.

Oh! She begins to howl quite horribly—but you run away, and the godless witch is miserably burnt to death.

You, however, run like lightning to Hansel, open his little stable, and cry, "Hansel, we are saved! The old witch is dead!"

Then Hansel springs like a bird from its cage when the door is opened. How you both rejoice and embrace each other and dance about! And as you no longer have any need to fear her, you go into the witch's house. In every corner, there stands chests full of pearls and jewels and even a **GOLDEN RING**.

"These are far better than pebbles!" says Hansel, and he thrusts into his pockets whatever can fit.

You say, "I, too, will take something home with me," and fill your pinafore full.

"But now we must be off," says Hansel, "that we may get out of the witch's forest."

When you have walked for two hours, you come to a great stretch of water.

"We cannot cross," says Hansel. "I see no foot-plank and no bridge."

"And there is also no ferry," you answer, "but a white duck is swimming there. If I ask, she will help us over."

Then you cry:

> "Little duck, little duck, dost thou see,
> Hansel and Gretel are waiting for thee?
> There's never a plank or bridge in sight,
> Take us across on thy back so white."

The duck comes to you. Hansel seats himself on its back and tells you to sit by him.

"No," you reply, "that will be too heavy for the little duck. She shall take us across, one after the other."

The good little duck does so, and when you are once safely across and have walked for a short time, the forest seems to be more and more familiar. At length, you see from afar your father's house. Then you both begin to run, rushing into the parlor and throwing yourselves around your father's neck.

The man had not known one happy hour since he had left you in the forest. The woman, however, is dead. You empty your pinafore until pearls and precious stones run about the room, and Hansel throws one handful after another out of his pocket to add to them.

Then all anxiety is at an end, and you live together in perfect happiness.

GO TO THE NEXT PAGE.

LITTLE RED-CAP

You are a dear little girl who is loved by everyone—
but most of all by your grandmother. There is nothing
that she would not give to you. Once, she gave you a
little cap of red velvet, which suited you so well that
you never wear anything else. So you are always called
"Little Red-Cap."

One day, your mother says, "Come, Little Red-Cap,
here is a piece of cake and a bottle of medicine. Take
them to your grandmother. She is ill and weak, and they
will do her good. Set out before it gets hot. Walk nicely
and quietly, and do not run off the path, or you may fall
and break the bottle. Then your grandmother will get
nothing. When you go into her room, don't forget to
say, 'Good morning,' and don't peep into every corner
before you do it."

"I will take great care," you promise your mother.

Your grandmother lives out in the wood, half a league from the village. As you enter the wood, a wolf meets you. You are not at all afraid of him.

"Good day, Little Red-Cap," says he.

"Thank you kindly, wolf."

"Where are you going so early, Little Red-Cap?"

"To my grandmother's."

"What have you got in your apron?"

"Cake and medicine. Yesterday was baking-day, so poor sick grandmother is to have something good, to make her stronger."

"Where does your grandmother live, Little Red-Cap?" asks the wolf.

"A good quarter of a league farther on in the wood. Her house stands under the three large oak-trees, and the nut-trees are just below. You surely must know it," you reply.

The wolf walks for a short time by your side and then says, "See, Little Red-Cap, how pretty the flowers are about here. Why do you not look around? I believe, too, that you do not hear how sweetly the little birds are singing. You walk gravely along as if you were going to school, while everything else out here is merry."

You raise your eyes, and you see the sunbeams dancing here and there through the trees, and pretty flowers growing everywhere. You think, *Suppose I take grandmother a fresh bunch of flowers. That would please her too. It is so early in the day that I shall still get there in good time.*

Your mother warned you not to run off the path, but the flowers are very near—and they will surely brighten your grandmother's mood. Can you spare the time to pick them?

Pick some flowers.

GO TO PAGE 77.

Stay on the path.

GO TO PAGE 67.

"I ask for the first sprig, dear father, that rubs against your hat on your way home," you say.

He buys for the two the fine clothes and pearls and diamonds they asked for. And on his way home, as he rides through a green copse, a sprig of hazel brushes against him. So he breaks it off, and when he gets home, he gives it to you.

Then you take it and go to your mother's grave and plant it there, and you cry so much that it is watered with your tears.

There it grows and becomes a fine tree, and soon a little bird comes and builds its nest upon the tree. It talks with you and watches over you and brings you whatever you wish for.

* * *

Now it happens that the king of the land holds a feast which is to last three days—and out of those who come to it, his son is to choose a bride for himself.

Your two sisters are asked to come. So they call you and say, "Now, comb our hair, brush our shoes, and tie our sashes, for we are going to dance at the king's feast."

Then you do as you are told. But when all is done, you cannot help crying, for you think to yourself, *I would have liked to go to the dance too.*

At last, you beg your step-mother to let you go.

"You! Cinderella?" says she. "You who have nothing to wear, no clothes at all, and who cannot even dance— you want to go to the ball?"

And when you keep on begging, to get rid of you, she says at last, "I will throw this basin full of peas into the ash heap. If you have picked them all out in two hours' time, you shall go to the feast too." Then she throws the peas into the ashes.

You run out the back door into the garden and cry:

"Hither, thither, through the sky,
turtle-doves and linnets, fly!
Blackbird, thrush, and chaffinch gay,
hither, thither, haste away!
One and all, come, help me quick!
Haste ye, haste ye: pick, pick, pick!"

First come two white doves and next two turtle-doves. After them, all the little birds under heaven come, and the little doves stoop their heads down and set to work, pick, pick, pick. Then the others begin to pick, pick, pick, and they pick out all the peas and put it into a dish.

At the end of one hour, the work is done, and all fly out again at the windows. Then you bring the dish to your step-mother.

But your step-mother says, "No, no! Indeed, you have no clothes and cannot dance. You shall not go."

And when you beg very hard to go, she says, "If you can, in one hour's time, pick two of these dishes of peas out of the ashes, you shall go." She shakes two dishes of peas into the ashes.

You go out into the garden at the back of the house and call as before, and all the birds come flying. In half an hour's time, all is done, and out they fly again.

And then you take the dishes to your step-mother, rejoicing to think that you should now go to the ball.

But she says, "It is all of no use; you cannot go. You have no clothes and cannot dance—and you would only put us to shame." And off she leaves with her two daughters to the feast.

Now when all are gone with nobody left at home, you go sorrowfully and sit down under the hazel-tree and cry, "Shake, shake, hazel-tree, gold and silver over me!"

Then your friend the bird flies out of the tree and brings a gold-and-silver dress for you and slippers of spangled silk. You put them on and follow your sisters to the feast.

But they do not recognize you. You look so fine and beautiful in your rich clothes.

The king's son soon comes up to you and takes you by the hand and dances with you and no one else—and he never leaves your hand.

When anyone else comes to ask you to dance, he says, "This lady is dancing with me."

You have such fun that you forget to check the time. When midnight arrives, you are still with the prince. Shall you continue to dance, or will you make haste and get back home?

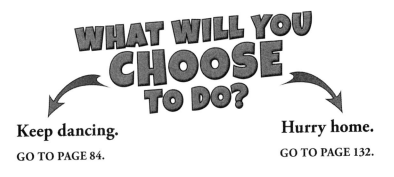

Keep dancing.

GO TO PAGE 84.

Hurry home.

GO TO PAGE 132.

Even though it is still midday, a dreadful darkness spreads across the land—across all lands. You watch helplessly as this world, this reality, crumbles and fades away, until all that is left is nothing.

GO TO PAGE 75.

"I'm sorry," you reply. "I cannot part with this ring. Will you not accept something else?"

"Then say you will give me," says the little man, "the first little child that you may have when you are queen."

That may never be, you think. As you know no other way to get your task done, you agree to do what he asks.

Round goes the wheel again to the old song, and the little man once more spins the heap into gold.

The king comes in the morning, and, finding all he wants, is forced to keep his word. So he marries you, and you really become queen.

* * *

At the birth of your first little child, you are very glad and forget the dwarf and what you had said. But one day, he comes into your room, where you are playing with your baby, and he puts you in mind of it.

Then you grieve sorely at your misfortune and say you will give him all the wealth of the kingdom if he will let you off, but in vain.

At last your tears soften him, and he says, "I will give you three days' grace, and if during that time you tell me my name, you shall keep your child."

You lie awake all night, thinking of all the odd names that you have ever heard. And you send messengers all over the land to find out new ones.

* * *

The next day, the little man comes, and you begin with Timothy, Ichabod, Benjamin, Jeremiah, and all the names you can remember.

To all and each of them, he says, "Madam, that is not my name."

GO TO THE NEXT PAGE.

The second day, you begin with all the comical names you could hear of: Bandy-Legs, Crook-Shanks, and so on.

But the little gentleman still says to every one of them, "Madam, that is not my name."

You are desperate, and you have but one last day, last chance, to discover his name. You can rely upon a trusted messenger to uncover this hidden word, or you can venture out and try to learn it yourself.

Send a messenger.

GO TO PAGE 128.

Find it yourself.

GO TO PAGE 76.

After many, many years there comes a king's son into a familiar land. That prince is you.

An old man tells you the story of a thicket of thorns and how a beautiful palace stands behind it and how a wonderful princess, called Briar Rose, lies in it asleep, with all her court. He tells, too, how he has heard from his grandfather that many, many princes have come and tried to break through the thicket, but they all stuck fast in it and died.

You say, "All this shall not frighten me. I will go and see this Briar Rose."

The old man tries to hinder you, but you are bent upon going.

Now that very day marks 100 years ago that Briar Rose fell into an enchanted sleep. As you come to the thicket, you see nothing but beautiful flowering shrubs, through which you go with ease. But they shut in after you as thick as ever.

You come at last to the palace. There in the court lie the dogs asleep. The horses stand in the stables, and on the roof sit the pigeons fast asleep, with their heads under their wings. And when you come into the palace, the flies are sleeping on the walls; the spit is standing still; the butler has a jug of water at his lips; the maid sits with a fowl in her lap ready to be plucked; and the cook in the kitchen still sleeps, as does the kitchen-boy.

You go on still farther, and all is so still that you can hear every breath you draw. At last you come to the old tower and open the door of the little room in which Briar Rose is, and there she lies, fast asleep on a couch by the window. She looks so beautiful that you cannot take your eyes off her.

At that moment, she opens her eyes and awakens and smiles upon you.

You go out together, and soon the king and queen also wake with all the court and gaze upon each other with great wonder. And the horses shake themselves, and the dogs jump up and bark; the pigeons take their heads from under their wings and look about and fly into the fields; the flies on the walls buzz again; the fire in the kitchen blazes up; around goes the jack and around goes the spit, with the goose for the king's dinner upon it. The butler finishes his drink; the maid goes on plucking the fowl; and the cook gives the boy the box on his ear.

You and Briar Rose are married, and the wedding feast is given. You live happily together all your lives.

GO TO PAGE 140.

RUMPELSTILTSKIN

By the side of a wood, in a country a long way off, runs a fine stream of water. Upon the stream, there stands a mill. The miller's house is close by, and you are the miller's daughter. You are very shrewd and clever.

The miller is so proud of you that he one day tells the king of the land, who comes and hunts in the wood, that you could spin gold out of straw.

Now this king is very fond of money. When he hears the miller's boast, his greediness is raised, and he sends for you to be brought before him. Then he leads you to a chamber in his palace where there is a great heap of straw, and he gives you a spinning-wheel.

He says, "All this must be spun into gold before morning, if you love your life."

In vain, you say, "It was only a silly boast of my father, for I can do no such thing as spin straw into gold."

The chamber door is locked, and you are left alone.

You sit down in one corner of the room and begin to bewail your hard fate.

All of a sudden, the door opens.

A droll-looking little man hobbles in. "Good morrow to you, my good lass. What are you weeping for?"

"Alas!" you say. "I must spin this straw into gold, and I know not how."

"What will you give me," says the hobgoblin, "to do it for you?"

"My necklace," you reply.

He takes you at your word and sits himself down to the wheel, and he whistles and sings:

"Round about, round about,
Lo and behold!
Reel away, reel away,
Straw into gold!"

And round about the wheel goes merrily. The work is quickly done, and the straw is all spun into gold.

When the king comes and sees this, he is greatly astonished and pleased. But his heart grows more greedy of gain, and he shuts you once again with a fresh task.

You know not what to do, and you sit down once more to weep.

But the dwarf soon opens the door and says, "What will you give me to do your task?"

"The bracelet on my wrist," you say.

So your little friend takes the bracelet and begins to work at the wheel again, and he whistles and sings:

> "Round about, round about,
> Lo and behold!
> Reel away, reel away,
> Straw into gold!"

Long before morning, all is done again.

The king is greatly delighted to see all this glittering treasure. But still he has not enough. So he takes you to a yet larger heap and says, "All this must be spun tonight—and if it is, you shall be my queen."

As soon as you are alone, the dwarf comes in and says, "What will you give me to spin gold for you this third time?"

"I have nothing left," you say.

"What about a **GOLDEN RING**?" he asks. "I will take that as payment for this task."

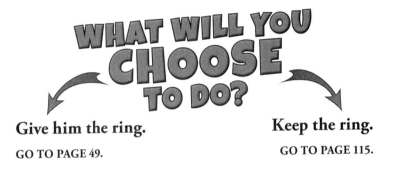

Give him the ring.

GO TO PAGE 49.

Keep the ring.

GO TO PAGE 115.

They cut down the tree but find no one upon it. And when they come back into the kitchen, there you lie in the ashes as usual—for you had slipped down on the other side of the tree and carried your beautiful clothes back to the bird at the hazel-tree, and then put on your little old frock.

GO TO THE NEXT PAGE.

The third day, when your father and step-mother and sisters are gone, you go again into the garden and say, "Shake, shake, hazel-tree, gold and silver over me!"

Your kind friend the bird brings a dress still finer than the former one and slippers which are all of gold.

The king's son dances with you alone. When anyone else asks you to dance, he says, "This lady is my partner."

Now when night comes and you want to go home, the king's son goes with you. But you manage to slip away from him, though in such a hurry that you drop your left **GOLDEN SLIPPER** upon the stairs.

So the prince takes the shoe and goes the next day to the king, his father, and says, "I will take for my wife the lady that this golden shoe fits."

Then both the sisters are overjoyed to hear this, for they have beautiful feet and have no doubt that they can wear the golden slipper.

As her mother stands by, the eldest goes first into the room where the slipper is and wants to try it on. But her big toe cannot go into it, and the shoe is altogether much too small for her.

Then the mother says, "Never mind, cut it off. When you are queen, you will not care about toes. You will not want to go on foot."

So the silly girl cuts her big toe off and squeezes the shoe on and goes to the king's son. Then he chooses her for his bride, and they ride away.

But on their way home, they have to pass by the hazel-tree that Cinderella had planted.

There sits a little dove on the branch, singing,

"Back again! Back again! Look to the shoe!
The shoe is too small, and not made for you!
Prince! Prince! Look again for thy bride,
For she's not the true one that sits by thy side."

Then the prince looks at her foot and sees by the blood that streams from it what a trick she has played on him.

So he brings the false bride back to her home and says, "This is not the right bride. Let the other sister try and put on the slipper."

Then she goes into the room and gets her foot into the shoe—all but the heel, which is too large. But her mother squeezes it in till the blood comes, and she takes her daughter to the king's son.

He rides away with her. But when they come to the hazel-tree, the little dove sits there still and sings as before. Then the king's son looks down and sees that the blood streams from the shoe.

So he brings her back again also. "This is not the true bride," says he to the father. "Have you no other daughters?"

Then Cinderella comes, and she takes her clumsy shoe off and puts on the golden slipper. It fits as if it had been made for her. And when he draws near and looks at her face, the prince knows her and says, "This is the right bride."

He takes Cinderella on his horse and rides away. And when they come to the hazel-tree, the white dove sings,

"Prince! Prince! Take home thy bride,
For she is the true one that sits by thy side!"

Yes.

GO TO PAGE 133.

No.

GO TO PAGE 114.

The third day, your most trusted messenger comes back and says, "I have traveled far without hearing of any other names. But as I was climbing a high hill, among the trees of the forest, where the fox and the hare bid each other goodnight, I saw a little hut. And before the hut burnt a fire. And round about the fire, a funny little dwarf was dancing upon one leg and singing:

"Merrily the feast I'll make.
Today I'll brew, tomorrow bake;
Merrily I'll dance and sing,
For next day will a stranger bring.
Little does my lady dream
Rumpelstiltskin is my name!"

When you hear this, you jump for joy.

* * *

As soon as the little man returns, you sit down upon your throne and call all your court around to enjoy the fun. The nurse stands by your side with the baby in her arms, as if it is quite ready to be given up.

Then the little man begins to chuckle at the thought of having the poor child, to take home with him to his hut in the woods.

He cries out, "Now, lady, what is my name?"

"Is it John?" you ask.

"No, madam!"

"Is it Tom?"

"No, madam!"

"Is it Jimmy?"

"It is not."

"Can your name be Rumpelstiltskin?" you say slyly.

"Some witch told you that! Some witch told you that!" cries the little man. He dashes his right foot in a rage so deep into the floor that he is forced to hold it with both hands to pull it out.

Then he makes the best of his way off, while the nurse laughs and the baby crows. And all the court jeers at him for having had so much trouble for nothing.

Together, they say, "We wish you a good morning and a merry feast, Mr. Rumplestiltskin!"

GO TO THE NEXT PAGE.

THE FROG-PRINCE

It is a fine evening, and you find yourself cast as a young princess. You put on your bonnet and clogs, and you go out to take a walk in the forest. When you come to a cool spring of water, you sit down to rest a while.

You have a **GOLDEN BALL** in your hand, which is your favorite plaything. You are always tossing it up into the air and catching it again as it falls. After a time, you throw it up so high that you miss catching it as it falls. The ball bounds away and rolls along the ground, till at last it falls down into the pond.

You look into the pond after your ball, but it is very deep—so deep that you cannot see the bottom of it.

You begin to bewail your loss, and say, "Alas! If I could only get my ball again, I would give all my fine clothes and jewels and everything I have in the world."

While you speak, a frog puts its head out of the water and says, "Princess, why do you weep so bitterly?"

"Alas!" you say. "What can you do for me, you nasty frog? My golden ball has fallen into the spring."

The frog says, "I want not your pearls and jewels and fine clothes. But if you will love me and let me live with you and eat from your plate and sleep upon your bed, I will bring you your ball again."

Can this frog be serious? And if it is, do you dare to make this deal? Your golden ball is important, but you know nothing about this frog.

Get the frog's help.

GO TO PAGE 98.

Send the frog away.

GO TO PAGE 80.

Oh, no, you think, *it's nearly midnight. I must get home with haste.*

You slip away from the king's son and run off towards home. The prince follows, so you dare not slow down. You plan to jump up into the pigeon-house and hide there, but it is difficult to run in your dress and silk slippers. You cannot make it to the pigeon-house in time, so you hide within the home of one Mr. Korbes.

You find the place empty, so you go to the fireplace to make a fire. But a cat throws all the ashes in your eyes, so you run to the kitchen to wash yourself. There, a duck splashes all the water in your face, and when you try to wipe yourself, an egg that had been rolled up in the towel breaks to pieces all over your face and eyes.

Then you are very angry and go to lie down on the bed. But when you rest your head on the pillow, a pin pokes into your cheek. At this you become quite upset and, jumping up, would run out of the house—but when you come to the door, a millstone falls down on your head and kills you on the spot.

GO TO PAGE 75.

The golden ball lifts into the air and floats before you. It starts to spin, moving faster and faster. As it does, it grows larger in size, and it glows.

Within seconds, the ball is bigger than you are and shines like the sun, too brightly to gaze upon directly.

The light is replaced by the figure of Allerleirauh, now covered in all kinds of fur.

"Your task is nearly complete," she says. "Our reality is all but saved. Just two steps remain. First, you must set right that which remains wrong."

* * *

You are a huntsman, just passing an old woman's house. You think to yourself, *How the old woman is snoring! I must just see if she wants anything.*

So you go into the room, and when you come to the bed, you see that a wolf is lying in it, asleep.

"Do I find you here, you old sinner!" you say. "I have long sought you!"

It occurs to you that the wolf might have devoured the grandmother and that she might still be saved. So you take a pair of scissors and begin to cut open the stomach of the sleeping wolf. When you have made two snips, you see the little red cap shining, and so you make two snips more.

The little girl springs out, crying, "Ah, how frightened I have been! How dark it was inside the wolf."

After that, the aged grandmother comes out alive also but scarcely able to breathe.

Red-Cap, however, quickly fetches great stones with which you all fill the wolf's belly.

When he wakes, he wants to run away, but the stones are so heavy that he collapses at once and falls dead.

The grandmother eats the cake, and she drinks the medicine and feels revived.

Red-Cap says, "As long as I live, I will never by myself leave the path, to run into the wood, when my mother has forbidden me to do so."

You draw off the wolf's skin and . . .

GO TO THE NEXT PAGE.

You are once more in the presence of Allerleirauh. She gently takes the wolf's skin from you and adds it to her costume. Then she gathers all the magical items you have collected. She places the golden ring upon her finger. The rest, she tucks safely away in a chest.

"Well done," she tells you. Her smile twinkles like starlight. "You have healed our wounded world and set our stories right again. For this, we owe you our lives, our very existence."

You bow humbly. "Is there another task to complete?"

She places her hand upon your shoulder. "Indeed, though it is a simple one. You must choose your 'happily ever after.'" She holds out both hands. In one is a tiny box made of glass. In the other, there lies a feather.

"Take one of these items," says Allerleirauh. "Hold it close to your heart."

Take the glass box.

GO TO PAGE 87.

Take the feather.

GO TO PAGE 118.

"Thank you, but I will honor my promise," you say. "It is the right thing to do."

The frog comes in and sleeps upon your pillow as before, till the morning breaks.

But when you wake on the following morning, you are astonished to see, instead of the frog, a handsome prince, standing at the head of your bed.

He tells you, "I had been enchanted by a spiteful fairy, who changed me into a frog. I had been fated so till some princess should take me out of the pond and let me eat from her plate and sleep upon her bed for three nights. You have broken this cruel charm."

A coach drives up, with eight beautiful horses, decked with plumes of feathers and a golden harness. Behind the coach rides the prince's servant, faithful Heinrich, who had bewailed the misfortunes of his dear master during his enchantment so long and so bitterly that his heart had nearly burst.

"You are always welcome in my father's kingdom," says the prince. Then he gets into the coach with eight horses and sets out, full of joy and merriment.

GO TO THE NEXT PAGE.

CINDERELLA

The wife of a rich man falls sick. When she feels that her end draws near, she calls you, her only daughter, to her bedside. She says, "Always be a good girl, and I will look down from heaven and watch over you."

Soon afterwards, she shuts her eyes and dies, and she is buried in the garden. You go every day to her grave and weep, and you are always good and kind to all around you. And the snow spreads a beautiful white covering over the grave.

By the time the sun has melted it away again, your father has married another wife. This new wife has two daughters of her own. They are fair in face but foul at heart, and it is now a sorry time for you.

"What does the good-for-nothing thing want in the parlor?" they say.

They take away your fine clothes and give you an old frock to put on, and they laugh at you and send you into the kitchen. Then you are forced to do hard work: to rise early—before daylight—to bring the water, to make the fire, to cook, and to wash. You have no bed to lie down on, but you are made to lie by the hearth among the ashes, and they call you Cinderella.

GO TO THE NEXT PAGE.

It happens once that your father goes to the fair and asks his wife's daughters what he should bring to them.

"Fine clothes," says the first.

"Pearls and diamonds," says the second.

"Now, child," he says to you, "what will you have?"

You try to live a simple life, so you don't want to ask for much. Maybe you should ask for a simple gift, such as something for the backyard or garden. However, you could use a bit of magic to change your fortunes. Perhaps you should ask for a **GOLDEN NECKLACE**—a bit of magic might come in handy later on.

Request a simple gift.

GO TO PAGE 110.

Ask for a golden gift.

GO TO PAGE 103.

CONGRATULATIONS!

You survived
The Grimms' Fairy Tales!

Choose your next adventure.

Available wherever books are sold

STEM ACTIVITY: THE TALLEST TOWER

Towers play an important role in *The Grimms' Fairy Tales*. For example, Rapunzel is locked away in one, and Briar Rose sleeps for 100 years in another. "The Tallest Tower" is a fun engineering-themed challenge that ties in nicely to the fairy tale theme.

WHAT YOU NEED:

Adult helper

Tall, stick-like building materials, such as
- dried spaghetti
- paper tower rolls
- pipe cleaners
- straws

Binding materials to connect the parts, such as
- jellybeans
- marshmallows
- paper clips
- tape

Any other creative materials you'd like to include

WHAT TO DO:

This activity is as simple as it is fun. Children can work alone or be divided into teams. Just instruct them to use the available materials—however they'd like—to create the tallest tower possible.

Typically, participants are given a time limit, such as 5–10 minutes. When time is up, the winner is the person or team with the tallest tower.

There are plenty of ways to vary this challenge. For example, you can allow each team to choose only two building materials, or you can assign different disadvantages to each team member, such as deciding that one person is not allowed to use their hands, another is not allowed to talk, and another is blindfolded.

Get creative. Have as much fun as you can imagine!

Safety Notice: *This activity is intended to be supervised by an adult, who must use his or her own judgment on the age-appropriateness of this activity. Do not let children under the age of 3 utilize any small items that could pose a choking hazard. By attempting this activity, you expressly agree to do so at your sole risk. For more information, please see the disclaimer on page 2.*

ABOUT THE AUTHORS

Jacob Grimm was born in Hanau, Germany, on January 4, 1785. His brother, **Wilhelm Grimm**, arrived 14 months later, on February 24, 1786. Their father died in 1796, and the brothers lived with very little money. Still, they were able to attend the University of Marburg, where they grew to love language and literature.

In 1808, they began working as librarians and started researching old folktales. They didn't create the fairy tales for which they are famous, but they gathered the stories through archives and by listening to storytellers.

In 1812, they published their collection of stories as *Kinder und Hausmärchen* (or *Children's and Household Tales*). The first edition was considered too violent, so the brothers released an edition that was much less gory.

They went on to publish Danish, Irish, and Norse folktales, and they spent years working on a German Dictionary before their deaths. Wilhelm passed away in 1859, and Jacob died in 1863.

Ryan Jacobson is an award-winning author of more than 60 books. His most popular works range from activity books and picture books to Choose Your Path books.